MARTYR

MARTYR

by Alan E. Nourse

"I can break him, split his Criterion Committee wide open *now* while there's still a chance, and open rejuvenation up to everybody...."

*

Four and one half hours after Martian sunset, the last light in the Headquarters Building finally blinked out.

Carl Golden stamped his feet nervously against the cold, cupping his cigarette in his hand to suck up the tiny spark of warmth. The night air bit his nostrils and made the smoke tasteless in the darkness. Atmosphere screens kept the oxygen in, all right—but they never kept the biting cold out. As the light disappeared he dropped the cigarette, stamping it sharply into darkness. Boredom vanished, and warm blood prickled through his shivering legs.

He slid back tight against the coarse black building front, peering across the road in the gloom.

It was the girl. He had thought so, but hadn't been sure. She swung the heavy stone door shut after her, glanced both left and right, and started down the frosty road toward the lights of the colony.

Carl Golden waited until she was gone. He glanced at his wrist-chrono, and waited ten minutes more. He didn't realize that he was trembling until he ducked swiftly across the road. Through the window of the low, one-story building he could see the lobby call-board, with the little colored studs all dark. He smiled in unpleasant satisfaction—no one was left in the building. It was routine, just like everything else in this god-forsaken hole. Utter, abysmal, trancelike routine. The girl was a little later than usual, probably because of the ship coming in tomorrow. Reports to get ready, supply requisitions, personnel recommendations—

—and the final reports on Armstrong's death. Mustn't forget that. The *real* story, the absolute, factual truth, without any nonsense. The reports that would go, ultimately, to Rinehart and only Rinehart, as all other important reports from the Mars Colony had been doing for so many years.

Carl skirted the long, low building, falling into the black shadows of the side wall. Halfway around he came to the supply chute, covered with a heavy moulded-stone cover.

Now?

It had taken four months here to know that he would have to do it this way. Four months of ridiculous masquerade—made idiotic by the incredible fact that everyone took him for exactly what he pretended to be, and never challenged him—not even Terry Fisher, who drunk or sober always challenged everything and everybody! But the four months had told on his nerves, in his reactions, in the hollows under his quick brown eyes. There was always the spectre of a slip-up, an aroused suspicion. And until he had the reports before his eyes, he couldn't fall back on Dan Fowler's name to save him. He had shook Dan's hand the night he had left, and Dan had said, "Remember, son—I don't know you. Hate to do it this way, but we can't risk it now—" And they couldn't, of course. Not until they knew, for certain, who had murdered Kenneth Armstrong.

They already knew why.

*

The utter stillness of the place reassured him; he hoisted up the chute cover, threw it high, and shinned his long body into the chute. It was a steep slide; he held on for an instant, then let go. Blackness gulped him down as the cover snapped closed behind him.

He struck hard and rolled. The chute opened into the commissary in the third deep-level of the building, and the place was black as the inside of a pocket. He tested unbroken legs with a sigh of relief, and limped across to where the door should be.

In the corridor there was some light—dim phosphorescence from the Martian night-rock lining the walls and tiling the floor. He walked swiftly, cursing the clack-clack his heels made on the ringing stone. When he reached the end of the corridor he tried the heavy door.

It gave, complaining. Good, good! It had been a quick, imperfect job of jimmying the lock, so obviously poor that it had worried him a lot—but why should they test it? There was still another door.

He stepped into the blackness again, started across the room as the door swung shut behind him.

A shoe scraped, the faintest rustle of sound. Carl froze. His own trouser leg? A trick of acoustics? He didn't move a muscle.

Then: "Carl?"

His pocket light flickered around the room, a small secretary's ante-room. It stopped on a pair of legs, a body, slouched down in the soft plastifoam chair—a face, ruddy and bland, with a shock of sandy hair, with quixotic eyebrows. "Terry! For Christ sake, what—"

The man leaned forward, grinning up at him. "You're late, Carl." His voice was a muddy drawl. "Should have made it sooner than this, sheems—seems to me."

MARTYR

Carl's light moved past the man in the chair to the floor. The bottle was standing there, still half full. "My god, you're *drunk!*"

"Course I'm drunk. Whadj-ya think, I'd sober up after you left me tonight? No thanks, I'd rather be drunk." Terry Fisher hiccupped loudly. "I'd always rather be drunk, around this place."

"All right, you've got to get out of here—" Carl's voice rose with bitter anger. Of all times, of *all* times—he wanted to scream. "How did you get in here? You've *got* to get out—"

"So do you. They're on to you, Carl. I don't think you know that, but they are." He leaned forward precariously. "I had a talk with Barness this morning, one of his nice 'spontaneous' chats, and he pumped the hell out of me and thought I was too drunk to know it. They're expecting you to come here tonight—"

Carl heaved at the drunken man's arm, frantically in the darkness. "Get *out* of here, Terry, or so help me—"

Terry clutched at him. "Didn't you hear me? They *know* about you. Personell supervisor! They think you're spying for the Eastern boys—they're starting a Mars colony too, you know. Barness is sure you're selling them info—" The man hiccupped again. "Barness is an ass, just like all the other Retreads running this place, but I'm not an ass, and you didn't fool me for two days—"

Carl gritted his teeth. How could Terry Fisher know? "For the last time—"

Fisher lurched to his feet. "They'll get you, Carl. They can try you and shoot you right on the spot, and Barness will do it. I had to tell you, you've walked right into it, but you might still get away if—"

8

It was cruel. The drunken man's head jerked up at the blow, and he gave a little grunt, then slid back down on the chair. Carl stepped over his legs, worked swiftly at the door beyond. If they caught him now, Terry Fisher was right. But in five more minutes—

The lock squeaked, and the door fell open. Inside he tore through the file cases, wrenched at the locked drawers in frantic haste, ripping the weak aluminum sheeting like thick tinfoil. Then he found the folder marked KENNETH ARMSTRONG on the tab.

Somewhere above him an alarm went off, screaming a mournful note through the building. He threw on the light switch, flooding the room with whiteness, and started through the papers, one by one, in the folder. No time to read. Flash retinal photos were hard to superimpose and keep straight, but that was one reason why Carl Golden was on Mars instead of sitting in an office back on Earth—

He flipped the last page, and threw the folder onto the floor. As he went through the door, he flipped out the light, raced with clattering footsteps down the corridor.

Lights caught him from both sides, slicing the blackness like hot knives. "*All right, Golden. Stop right there.*"

Dark figures came out of the lights, ripped his clothing off without a word. Somebody wrenched open his mouth, shined a light in, rammed coarse cold fingers down into his throat. Then: "All right, you bastard, up stairs. Barness wants to see you."

They packed him naked into the street, hurried him into a three-wheeled ground car. Five minutes later he was wading through frosty dust into another building, and Barness was glaring at him across the room.

MARTYR

*

Odd things flashed through Carl's mind. You seldom saw a Repeater get really angry—but Barness was angry. The man's young-old face (the strange, utterly ageless amalgamation of sixty years of wisdom, superimposed by the youth of a twenty-year-old) had unaccustomed lines of wrath about the eyes and mouth. Barness didn't waste words. "What did you want down there?"

"Armstrong." Carl cut the word out almost gleefully. "And I got it, and there's nothing you or Rinehart or anybody else in between can do about it. I don't know *what* I saw yet, but I've got it in my eyes and in my cortex, and you can't touch it."

"You stupid fool, we can *peel* your cortex," Barness snarled.

"Well, you won't. You won't dare."

Barness glanced across at the officer who had brought him in. "Tommy—"

"Dan Fowler won't like it," said Carl.

Barness stopped short, blinking. He took a slow breath. Then he sank down into his chair. "Fowler" he said, as though dawn were just breaking.

"That's right. He sent me up here. I've found what he wants. Shoot me now, and when they probe you Dan will know I found it, and you won't be around for another rejuvenation."

Barness looked suddenly old. "What did he want?"

"The truth about Armstrong. Not the 'accident' story you fed to the teevies.... *Tragic End for World Hero, Died With His Boots On*". Dan wanted the truth. Who killed him. Why this colony is grinding down from compound low to stop, and turning men like Terry Fisher into alcoholic bums. Why this colony is turning into a glorified, super-refined Birdie's Rest for old men.

10

But mostly who killed Armstrong, how he was murdered, who gave the orders. And if you don't mind, I'm beginning to get cold."

"And you got all that," said Barness.

"That's right."

"You haven't read it, though."

"Not yet. Plenty of time for that on the way back."

Barness nodded wearily, and motioned the guard to give Carl his clothes. "I think you'd better read it tonight. Maybe it'll surprise you."

Golden's eyes widened. Something in the man's voice, some curious note of defeat and hopelessness, told him that Barness was not lying. "Oh?"

"Armstrong didn't have an accident, that's true. But nobody murdered him, either. Nobody gave any orders, to anybody, from anybody. Armstrong put a bullet through his head—quite of his own volition."

II

"All right, Senator," the young red-headed doctor said. "You say you want it straight—that's how you're going to get it." Moments before, Dr. Moss had been laughing. Now he wasn't laughing. "Six months, at the outside. Nine, if you went to bed tomorrow, retired from the Senate, and lived on tea and crackers. But where I'm sitting I wouldn't bet a plugged nickel that you'll be alive a month from now. If you think I'm joking, you just try to squeeze a bet out of me."

Senator Dan Fowler took the black cigar from his mouth, stared at the chewed-up end for a moment, and put it back in again. He had had something exceedingly witty all ready to say at this point in the examination; now it didn't seem to be too funny. If Moss had been a mealy-mouthed quack like the last Doc he had seen, okay. But Moss wasn't. Moss was obviously not impressed by the old man sitting across the desk from him, a fact which made Dan Fowler just a trifle uneasy. And Moss knew his turnips.

Dan Fowler looked at the doctor and said, "Garbage."

The red-headed doctor shrugged. "Look, Senator—sometimes a banana is a banana. I know heart disease, and I know how it acts. I know that it kills people if they wait too long. And when you're dead, no rejuvenation lab is going to bring you back to life again."

"Oh, hell! Who's dying?" Fowler's grey eyebrows knit in the old familiar scowl, and he bit down hard on the cigar. "Heart disease! So I get a little pain now and then—sure it won't last forever, and when it gets bad I'll come in and take the full treatment. But I can't do it now!" He spread his hands in a violent gesture. "I only came in here because my daughter dragged me. My heart's doing fine—I've been working an eighteen hour day for forty years now, and I can do it for another year or two—"

"But you have pain," said Dr. Moss.

"So? A little twinge, now and then."

"Whenever you lose your temper. Whenever anything upsets you."

"All right—a twinge."

"Which makes you sit down for ten or fifteen minutes. Which doesn't go away with one nitro-tablet any more, so you have to take two, and sometimes three—right?"

*

Dan Fowler blinked. "All right, sometimes it gets a little bad—"

"And it used to be only once or twice a month, but now it's almost every day. And once or twice you've blacked clean out for a while, and made your staff work like demons to cover for you and keep it off the teevies, right?"

"Say, who's been talking to you?"

"Jean has been talking to me."

"Can't even trust your own daughter to keep her trap shut." The Senator tossed the cigar butt down in disgust. "It happened once, yes. That god damned Rinehart is enough to make anybody black out." He thrust out his jaw and glowered at Dr. Moss as though it were all *his* fault. Then he grinned. "Oh, I know you're right, Doc. It's just that this is the wrong *time*. I can't take two months out now—there's too much to be done between now and the middle of next month."

"Oh, yes. The Hearings. Why not turn it over to your staff? They know what's going on."

"Nonsense. They know, but not like I know. After the Hearings, fine—I'll come along like a lamb. But now—"

Dr. Moss reddened, slammed his fist down on the desk. "Dammit, man, are you blind and deaf? Or just plain stupid? Didn't you hear me a moment ago? *You may not live through the Hearings.* You could *go*, just like that, any minute. But this is 2134 A.D., not the middle ages. It would be so utterly, hopelessly pointless to let that happen—"

Fowler champed his cigar and scowled. "After it was done I'd have to Free-Agent for a year, wouldn't I?" It was an accusation.

"You *should*. But that's a formality. If you want to go back to what you were doing the day you came from the Center—"

MARTYR

"Yes, *if*! But supposing I didn't? Supposing I was all changed?"

The young doctor looked at the old man shrewdly. Dan Fowler was 56 years old—and he looked forty. It seemed incredible even to Moss that the man could have done what he had done, and look almost as young and fighting-mad now as he had when he started. Clever old goat, too—but Dan Fowler's last remark opened the hidden door wide. Moss smiled to himself. "You're afraid of it, aren't you, Senator?"

"Of rejuvenation? Nonsense."

"But you are. You aren't the only one—it's a pretty frightening thing. Cash in the old model, take out a new one, just like a jet racer or a worn out talk-writer. Only it isn't machinery, it's your body, and your life." Dr. Moss grinned. "It scares a man. *Rejuvenation* isn't the right word, of course. Aside from the neurones, they take away every cell in your body, one way or another, and give you new ones. A hundred and fifty years ago Cancelmo and Klein did it on a dog, and called it *sub-total prosthesis*. A crude job—I've seen their papers and films. Vat-grown hearts and kidneys, revitalized vascular material, building up new organ systems like a patchwork quilt, coaxing new tissues to grow to replace old ones—but they got a living dog out of it, and that dog lived to the ripe old age of 37 years before he died."

*

Moss pushed back from his desk, watching Dan Fowler's face. "Then in 1992 Nimrock tried it on a man, and almost got himself hanged because the man died. That was a hundred and forty-two years ago. And then while he was still on trial, his workers completed the second job, and the man *lived*, and oh, how the jig changed for Nimrock!"

The doctor shrugged. As he talked, Dan Fowler sat silent, chewing his cigar furiously. But listening—he was listening, all right. "Well, it was crude, then," Moss said. "It's not so crude any more." He pointed to a large bronze plaque hanging on the office wall. "You've seen that before. Read it."

Dan Fowler's eyes went up to the plaque. A list of names. At the top words said, *These ten gave life to Mankind.*

Below it were the names:

Martin Aronson, Ph. D. Education

Thomas Bevalaqua Literature and Art

Chauncy Devlin Music

Frederick A. Kehler, M. S. Engineering

William B. Morse, L. L. D. Law

Rev. Hugh H. F. Norton Philosophy and Theology

Jacob Prowsnitz, Ph. D. History

Arthur L. Rodgers, M. D. Medicine

Carlotta Sokol, Ph. D. Sociopsychology

Harvey Tatum Business

"I know," said Dan Fowler. "June 1st, 2005. They were volunteers."

"Ten out of several dozen volunteers," Moss amended. "Those ten were chosen by lot. Already people were dreaming of what sub-total prosthesis could do. It could preserve the great minds, it could compound the accumulated wisdom of one lifetime with another lifetime—and maybe more. Those ten people—representing ten great fields of study—risked their lives. Not to live forever—just to see if rejuvenation could really preserve their minds in newly built bodies. All of them were old, older than you are, Senator, some were sicker than you, and all of them were afraid. But seven of the ten are *still alive today*, a hundred and thirty years later. Rodgers died in a jet crash. Tatum died of neuro-toxic virus, because we couldn't do anything to rebuild neurones in those days. Bevalaqua suicided. The rest are still alive, after two more rejuvenations."

"Fine," said Dan Fowler. "I still can't do it now."

"That was just ten people," Moss cut in. "It took five years to get ready for them. But now we can do five hundred a year—only five hundred select individuals, to live on instead of dying. And you've got the gall to sit there and tell me you don't have the time for it!"

*

The old man rose slowly, lighting another cigar. "It could be five thousand a year. That's why I don't have the time. Fifteen thousand, fifty thousand. We could do it—but we're not doing it. Walter Rinehart's been rejuvenated—twice already! *I'm* on the list because I shouted so loud they didn't dare leave me off. But *you're* not on it. Why not? You could be. Everybody could be."

Dr. Moss spread his hands. "The Criterion Committee does the choosing."

"*Rinehart's* criteria! Only five hundred a year. Use it for a weapon. Build power with it. Get a strangle-hold on it, and never, never let it go." The Senator leaned across the desk, his eyes bright with anger. "I haven't got time to stop what I'm doing now—because I can *stop* Rinehart, if I only live that long, I can break him, split his Criterion Committee wide open *now* while there's still a chance, and open rejuvenation up to everybody instead of five hundred lucky ones a year. I can stop him because I've dug at him and dug at him for twenty-nine years, and shouted and screamed and fought and made people

16

listen. And if I fumble now, it'll all be down the drain, finished, washed up.

"If that happens, *nobody* will ever stop him."

There was silence in the room for a moment. Then Moss spread his hands. "The hearings are that critical, eh?"

"I'm afraid so."

"Why has it got to be *your* personal fight? Other people could do it."

"They'd fumble it. They'd foul it up. Senator Libby fouled it up once already, a long time ago. Rinehart's lived for a hundred and nineteen years, and he's learning new tricks every year. I've only lived fifty-six of them, but I know his tricks. I can beat him."

"But why *you*?"

"Somebody's got to do it. My card is on top."

A 'phone buzzer chirped. "Yes, he's here." Dr. Moss handed Dan the receiver. A moment later the Senator was grinning like a cat struggling into his overcoat and scarf. "Sorry, Doc—I know what you tell me is true, and I'm no fool. If I have to stop, I'll stop."

"Tomorrow, then."

"Not tomorrow. One of my lads is back from the Mars Colony. Tomorrow we pow-wow—but hard. After the hearings, Doc. And meanwhile, keep your eye on the teevies. I'll be seeing you."

The door clicked shut with a note of finality, and Dr. David Moss stared at it gloomily. "I hope so," he said. But nobody in particular heard him.

MARTYR

III

A Volta two-wheeler was waiting for him outside. Jean drove off down the drive with characteristic contempt for the laws of gravity when Dan had piled in, and Carl Golden was there, looking thinner, more gaunt and hawk-like than ever before, his brown eyes sharp under his shock of black hair, his long, thin aquiline nose ("If you weren't a Jew you'd be a discredit to the Gentiles," Dan Fowler had twitted him once, years before, and Carl had looked down his long, thin, aquiline nose, and sniffed, and let the matter drop, because until then he had never been sure whether his being a Jew had mattered to Dan Fowler or not, and now he knew, and was quite satisfied with the knowledge) and the ever-present cigarette between thin, sensitive fingers. Dan clapped him on the shoulder, and shot a black look at his daughter, relegating her to an indescribable Fowler limbo, which was where she belonged, and would reside until Dan got excited and forgot how she'd betrayed him to Dr. Moss, which would take about ten or fifteen minutes all told. Jean Fowler knew her father far too well to worry about it, and squinted out the window at the afternoon traffic as the car skidded the corner into the Boulevard Throughway, across the river toward home. "God damn it, boy, you could have *wired* me at least. One of Jean's crew spotted the passage list, so I knew you'd left, and got the hearing moved up to next month—"

Carl scowled. "I thought it was all set for February 15th."

Dan chuckled. "It was. But I was only waiting for you, and got the ball rolling as soon as I knew you were on your way. Dwight McKenzie is still writing the Committee's business calendar, of course, and he didn't like it a bit, but he couldn't find any solid reason why it *shouldn't* be set ahead. And I think our good friend Senator Rinehart is probably wriggling on the stick about now, just on the shock value of the switch. Always figure in the shock value of everything you do, my boy—it pays off more than you'd ever dream—"

Carl Golden shook his head. "I don't like it, Dan."

"What, the switch in dates?"

"The switch. I wish you hadn't done that."

"But why? Look, son, I know that with Ken Armstrong dead our whole approach has to be changed—it's going to be trickier, but it might even work out better. The Senate knows what's been going on between Rinehart and me, and so does the President. They know elections are due next June. They know I want a seat on his Criterion Committee before elections, and they know that to get on it I'll do my damnedest to unseat him. They know I've shaken him up, that he's scared of me. Okay, fine. With Armstrong there to tell how he was chosen for Retread back in '87, we'd have had Rinehart running for his life...."

"But you don't," Carl cut in flatly, "and that's that."

"What, are you crazy, son? *I needed Armstrong, bad.* Rinehart knew it, and had him taken care of. It was fishy—it stunk from here to Mars, but Rinehart covered it up fast and clean. But with the stuff you got up in the Colony, we can charge Rinehart with murder, and the whole Senate knows his motive already. He didn't *dare* to let Armstrong testify."

*

Carl was shaking his head sadly.

"Well, what's wrong?"

"You aren't going to like this, Dan. Rinehart's clean. Armstrong comitted suicide."

MARTYR

Fowler's mouth fell open, and he sat back hard. "Oh, no."

"Sorry."

"Ken Armstrong? Suicided?" He shook his head helplessly, groping for words. "I—I—oh, Jesus. I don't believe it. If Ken Armstrong suicided, I'm the Scarlet Whore of Babylon."

"Well, we'll try to keep *that* off the teevies."

"There's no chance that you're wrong," said the old man.

Carl shook his head. "There's plenty that's funny about that Mars Colony, but Armstrong's death was suicide. Period. Even Barness didn't understand it."

Sharp eyes went to Carl's face. "What's funny about the Colony?"

Carl shrugged, and lit a cigarette. "Hard to say. This was my first look, I had nothing to compare it with. But there's *something* wrong. I always thought the Mars Colony was a frontier, a real challenge—you know, Man against the Wilderness, and all that. Saloons jammed on Saturday nights with rough boys out to get some and babes that had it to give. A place that could take Earthbound softies and toughen them up in a week, working to tame down the desert—"

His voice trailed off. "They've got a saloon, all right—but everybody just comes in quietly and gets slobbery drunk. Met a guy named Fisher, thought the same thing I did when he came up five years ago. A real go-getter, leader type, lots of ideas and the guts to put them across. Now he's got a hob-nail liver and he came back here on the ship with me, hating Mars and everything up there, most of all himself. Something's wrong up there, Dan. Maybe that's why Armstrong bowed out."

The Senator took a deep breath. "Not a man like Ken Armstrong. Why, I used to worship him when I was a kid. I was

20

ten when he came back to Earth for his second Retread." The old man shook his head. "I wanted to go back to Mars with him—I actually packed up to run away, until dear brother Paul caught me and squealed to Dad. Imagine."

"I'm sorry, Dan."

The car whizzed off the Throughway, and began weaving through the residential areas of Arlington. Jean swung under an arched gate, stopped in front of a large greystone house of the sort they hadn't built for a hundred years. Dan Fowler stared out at the grey November afternoon. "Well, then we're really on thin ice at the Hearings. We can still do it. It'll take some steam-rollering, but we can manage it." He turned to the girl. "Get Schirmer on the wire as soon as we get inside. I'll go over Carl's report for whatever I can find. Tell Schirmer if he wants to keep his job as Coordinator of the Medical Center next year, he'd better have all the statistics available on all rejuvenated persons past and present, in my office tomorrow morning."

Jean gave her father a queer look. "Schirmer's waiting for you inside right now."

"Oh? Why?"

"He wouldn't say. Nothing to do with politics, he said. Something about Paul."

*

Nathan Shirmer was waiting in the library, sipping a brandy and pretending to scan a Congressional Record in the viewer-box. He looked up, bird-like, as Dan Fowler strode in. "Well, Nate. Sit down, sit down. I see you're into my private stock already, so I won't offer you any. What's this about my brother?"

21

MARTYR

Schirmer coughed into his hand. "Why—Dan, I don't quite know how to tell you this. He was in Washington this afternoon—"

"Of course he was. He was supposed to go to the Center—" Dan broke off short, whirling on Schirmer. "Wait a minute! There wasn't a slip-up on this permit?"

"Permit?"

"For rejuvention, you ass! He's on the Starship Project, coordinating engineer of the whole works out there. He's got a fair place on the list coming to him three ways from Sunday. Follmer put the permit through months ago, and Paul has just been diddling around getting himself clear so he could come in—"

The little Coordinator's eyes widened. "Oh, there wasn't anything wrong on *our* side, if that's what you mean. The permit was perfectly clear, the doctors were waiting for him. It was nothing like that."

"Then what was it like?"

Nathan Schirmer wriggled, and tried to avoid Dan's eyes. "Your brother refused it. He laughed in our faces, and told us to go to hell, and took the next jet back to Nevada. All in one afternoon."

The vibration of the jet engines hung just at perception level, nagging and nagging at Dan Fowler, until he threw his papers aside with a snarl of disgust, and peered angrily out the window.

They were high, and moving fast. Far below was a tiny spot of light in the blackness. Pittsburgh. Maybe Cleveland. It didn't matter which. Jets traveled at such-and-such a rate of speed; they left at such-and-such a time and arrived elsewhere at such-and-such a time later. He could worry, or he could

22

not-worry. The jet would bring him down in Las Vegas in exactly the same time, to the second, either way. Another half-hour taxi ride over dusty desert roads would bring him to the glorified quonset hut his brother called home. Nothing Dan Fowler could do would hurry the process of getting there.

Dan had called, and received no answer.

He had talked to the Las Vegas authorities, and even gotten Lijinsky at the Starship, and neither of them knew anything. The police said yes, they would check at Dr. Fowler's residence, if he wasn't out at the Ship, and check back. But they hadn't checked back, and that was two hours ago. Meanwhile, Carl had chartered him a plane.

God damn Paul to three kinds of hell. Of all miserable times to start playing games, acting like an imbecile child! And the work and sweat Dan had gone through to get that permit, to buy it beg it, steal it, gold-plate it. Of course the odds were good that Paul would have gotten it without a whisper from Dan—he was high on the list, he was critical to Starship, and certainly Starship was critical enough to rate. But Dan had gone out on a limb, way out—The Senator's fist clenched, and he drummed it helplessly on the empty seat, and felt a twinge of pain spread up his chest, down his arm. He cursed, fumbled for the bottle in his vest pocket. God damned heart and god damned brother and god damned Rinehart—did *everything* have to split the wrong way? Now? Of all times of all days of all his fifty-six years of life, *now?*

All right, Dan. Cool, boy. Relax. Shame on you. Can't you quit being selfish just for a little while? Dan didn't like the idea as it flickered through his mind, but then he didn't like anything too much right then, so he forced the thought back for a rerun.

23

MARTYR

Big Dan Fowler, *Senator* Dan Fowler, Selfish Dan Fowler loves Dan Fowler mostly.

Poor Paul.

*

The words had been going through his mind like a silly chant since the first moment he had seen Nate Schirmer in the library. Poor Paul. Dan did all right for himself, he did—made quite a name down in Washington, you know, a fighter, a real fighter. The Boy with the Golden Touch (joke, son, laugh now). Everything he ever did worked out with him on top, somehow. Paul was different. Smart enough, plenty of the old gazoo, but he never had Dan's drive. Bad breaks, right down the line. Kinda tough on a guy, with a comet like Dan in the family. Poor Paul.

He let his mind drift back slowly, remembering little things, trying to spot the time, the single instant in time, when he stopped fighting Paul and started feeling sorry for him. It had been different, years ago. Paul was the smart one, all right. Never had Dan's build but he could think rings around him. Dan was always a little slow—never forgot anything he learned, but he learned slow. Still, there were ways to get around that—

Dad and Mom always liked Paul the best (their first boy, you know) and babied him more, and that was decidedly tougher to get around—Still there were ways.

Like the night the prize money came from the lottery, when he and Paul had split a ticket down the middle. How old was he then—ten? Eleven? And Paul was fifteen. He'd grubbed up the dollar polishing cars, and met Paul's dollar halfway, never dreaming the thing would pay off. And when it did! Oh, he'd never forget that night. He wanted the jet-racer. The ticket paid two thousand, a hell of a lot of cash for a pair of boys—and the two thousand would buy the racer. He'd been so excited tears had poured down his face.... But Paul had said no. Split it even, just like the ticket, Paul had said. There were hot words, and pleading, and threats, and Paul had just laughed at him until he got so mad he wanted to kill him with only his fists. Bad mistake, that. Paul was skinny, not much muscle, read books all the time it looked like a cinch. But Paul had five years on him that he hadn't counted on. Important five years. Paul connected with just one—enough to lay Dan flat on his back with a concussion and a broken jaw, and that, my boy, was that.

Almost.

Dan had won the fight, of course. It was the broken jaw that did it, that night, later the fight Mom and Dad had, worse than usual, a cruel one, low blows, mean—But Dan got his racer, on the strength of the broken jaw. That jaw had done him a lot of good. Never grew quite right after that, got one of the centers of ossification, the doc had said, and Dan had been god's gift to the pen-and-brush men with that heavy, angular jaw—a fighter's jaw, they called it.

*

That started it, of course. He knew then that he could beat Paul. Good to know. But never *sure* of it, always having to prove it. The successes came, and always he let Paul know about them, watched Paul's face like a cat. And Paul would squirm, and sneer, and tell Dan that in the end it was brains that would pay off. Sour grapes, of course. If Paul had ever squared off to him again, man to man, they might have had it over with. But Paul just seemed content to sit and quietly hate him.

MARTYR

Like the night he broke the Universalists in New Chicago, at the hundred-dollar-a-plate dinner. He'd told them, that night. That was the night they'd cold-shouldered him, and put Libby up to run for Mayor. Oh, he'd raised a glorious stink that night—he'd never enjoyed himself so much in his life, turning their whole twisted machine right over to the public on a silver platter. Cutting loose from the old crowd, appointing himself a committee of one to nominate himself on an Independent Reform ticket, campaign himself, and elect himself. A whippersnapper of thirty-two. Paul had been amused by it all, almost indulgent. "You *do* get melodramatic, don't you, Dan? Well, if you want to cut your own throat, that's your affair." And Dan had burned, and told Paul to watch the teevies, he'd see a thing or two, and he did, all right. He remembered Paul's face a few months later, when Libby conceded at 11:45 PM on election night, and Dan rode into office with a new crowd of livewires who were ready to help him plow into New Chicago and clean up that burg like it'd never been cleaned up. And the sweetest part of the victory pie had been the look on Paul's face that night—

So they'd fought, and he'd won and rubbed it in, and Paul had lost, and hated him for it, until that mysterious day—when had it really happened?—when "that big-brained brother of mine" changed subtly into "Christ, man, quit floundering! Who wants engineers? They're all over the place, you'll starve to death" and then finally, to "poor Paul."

When had it happened? Why?

Dan wondered, suddenly, if he had ever really forgiven Paul that blow to the jaw—

Perhaps.

He shook himself, scowling into the plastiglass window blackness. Okay, they'd fought it out. Always jolly, always making it out to be a big friendly game, only it never was a game. He knew how much he owed to Paul. He'd known it with growing concern for a lot of years. And now if he had to drag him back to Washington by the hair, he'd drag the silly fool—

IV

They didn't look very much alike. There was a spareness about Paul—a tall, lean, hungry-looking man, with large soft eyes that hid their anger and a face that was lined with tiredness and resignation. A year ago, when Dan had seen him last, he had looked a young 60, closer to 45; now he looked an old, old 61. How much of this was the cancer Dan didn't know. The pathologist had said: "Not a very malignant tumor right now, but you can never tell when it'll blow up. He'd better be scheduled at the Center, if he's got a permit—"

But some of it was Paul, just Paul. The house was exactly as Dan had expected it would be (though he had never been inside this house since Paul had come to Starship Project fifteen years ago)—stuffy, severe, rather gloomy, rooms packed with bookshelves, drawing boards, odds and ends of papers and blueprints and inks, thick, ugly furniture from the early 2000's, a cluttered, improvised, helter-skelter barn of a testing-lab, with modern equipment that looked lost and alien scattered among the mouldering junk of two centuries.

"Get your coat," said Dan. "It's cold outside. We're going back to Washington."

"Have a drink." Paul waved him toward the sideboard. "Relax. Your pilot needs a rest."

MARTYR

"Paul, I didn't come here to play games. The games are over now."

Paul poured a brandy with deliberation. Handed Dan one, sipped his own. "Good brandy," he murmured. "Wish I could afford more of it."

"*Paul.* You're going with me."

The old man shrugged with a little tired smile. "I'll go with you if you insist, of course. But I'm not going."

"Do you know what you're saying?"

"Perfectly."

"Paul, you don't just say 'Thanks, but I don't believe I'll have any' when they give you a rejuvenation permit. *Nobody* refuses rejuvenation. Why, there are a million people out there begging for a place on the list. It's *life*, Paul. You can't just turn it down—"

"This *is* good brandy," said Paul. "Would you care to take a look at my lab, by the way? Not too well equipped, but sometimes I can work here better than—"

Dan swung on his brother viciously. "I will tell you what I'm going to do," he grated, hitting each word hard, like knuckles rapping the table. "I'm going to take you to the plane. If you won't come, my pilot and I will drag you. When we get to Washington, we'll take you to the Center. If you won't sign the necessary releases, I'll forge them. I'll bribe two witnesses who will swear in the face of death by torture that they saw you signing. I'll buy out the doctors that can do the job, and if they won't do it, I'll sweat them down until they *will*."

*

He slammed the glass down on the table, feeling his heart pounding in his throat, feeling the pain creep up. "I've got lots of things on lots of people, and I can get things done when I want them done. People don't fool with me in Washington any more, because when they do they get their fingers burned off at the knuckles. For Christ sake, Paul, I knew you were stubborn but I didn't think you were block-headed stupid!"

Paul shrugged, apologetically. "I'm impressed, Dan. Really."

"You don't think I can do it?" Dan roared.

"Oh, no doubt you *could*. But such a lot of trouble for an unwilling victim. And I'm your brother, Dan. Remember?"

Dan Fowler spread his hands in defeat, then sank down in the chair. "Paul, tell me *why*."

"I don't want to be rejuvenated." As though he were saying, "I don't want any sugar in my coffee."

"Why not? If I could only see why, if I knew what was going through your mind, maybe I could understand. But I can't."

Dan looked up at Paul, practically pleading. "You're *needed*. I had a tape from Lijinsky last month—do you know what he said? He said why couldn't you have come to Starship ten years earlier? Nobody knows that ship like you do, you're making it go. That ship can take men to the stars, now, with rejuvenation, and the same men can come back again to find the same people waiting for them when they get here. They can *live* that long, now. We've been tied down to seventy years of life, to a tight little universe of one sun and nine planets for thousands of years. Well, we can change that now. We can go out. That's what your work can do for us." He stared helplessly at his brother. "You could go out on that ship you're building, Paul. You've always wanted to. *Why not?*"

29

MARTYR

Paul looked across at him for a long moment. There was pity in his eyes. There was also hatred there, and victory, long awaited, bitterly won. "Do you really want me to tell you?"

"I want you to tell me."

Then Paul told him. It took about ten minutes. It was not tempered with mercy.

It split Dan Fowler's world wide open at the seams.

*

"You've been talking about the Starship," said Paul Fowler. "All right, that's as good a starting place as any. I came to Starship Project—what was it, fifteen years ago? Almost sixteen, I guess. This was my meat. I couldn't work well with people, I worked with *things*, processes, ideas. I dug in hard on Starship. I loved it, dreamed it, lived with it. I had dreams in those days. Work hard, make myself valuable here, maybe I'd *get* rejuvenation, so I could work more on Starship. I believed everything you just said. Alpha Centauri, Arcturus, Vega, anywhere we wanted to go—and I could go along! It wouldn't be long, either. We had Lijinsky back with us after his rejuvenation, directing the Project, we had Keller and Stark and Eddie Cochran—great men, the men who had pounded Starship Project into reality, took it out of the story books and made the people of this country want it bad enough to pay for it. Those men were back now—new men, rebuilt bodies, with all their knowledge and experience preserved. Only now they had something even more precious than life: *time*. And I was part of it, and I too could have time."

Paul shook his head, slowly, and sank back into the chair. His eyes were very tired. "A dream, nothing more. A fantasy. It took me fifteen years to learn what a dream it was. Not even a suspicion at first—only a vague puzzlement, things happening that I couldn't quite grasp. Easy to shrug off, until it got too obvious. Not a matter of wrong decisions, really. The decisions were right, but they were in the wrong places. Something about Starship Project shifting, changing somehow. Something being lost. Slowly. Nothing you could nail down, at first, but growing month by month.

"Then one night I saw what it was. That was when I equipped the lab here, and proved to myself that Starship Project was a dream."

*

He spread his hands and smiled at Dan like a benign old Chips to a third-form schoolboy. "The Starship isn't going to Alpha Centauri or anywhere else. It's not going to leave the ground. I thought I'd live long enough to launch that ship and be one of its crew. Well, I won't. That ship wouldn't leave the ground if I lived a million years."

"Garbage," said Dan Fowler succinctly.

"No, Dan. Not garbage. Unfortunately, we sometimes have to recognize our dreams as dreams, and look reality right square in the face. Starship Project is dying. Our whole civilization is dying. Nimrock drove the first nail into the coffin a hundred and thirty years ago—lord, if they'd only hanged him when his first rejuvenation failed! But that would only have delayed it. Now we're dying, slowly right now, but soon it will be fast, very fast. And do you know who's getting set to land the death-blow?" He smiled sadly across at his brother. "You are, Dan."

Dan Fowler sprang from his chair with a roar. "My god, Paul, you're *sick*! Of all the idiot's delights I ever heard, I—I—oh,

Jesus." He stood shaking, groping for words, staring at his brother.

"You said you wanted me to tell you."

"Tell me! Tell me what?" Dan took a trembling breath, and sat down, visibly, gripping himself. "All right, all right, I heard what you said—you must mean something, but I don't know what. Let's be reasonable. Let's forget philosophy and semantics and concepts and all the frills for just a minute and talk about facts, huh? *Just facts.*"

"All right, facts," said Paul. "Kenneth Armstrong wrote MAN ON MARS in 2028—he was fifty-seven years old then, and he hadn't been rejuvenated yet. Fundamentally a good book, analyzing his first Mars Colony, taking it apart right down to the silk undies, to show why it had failed so miserably, and why the next one could succeed if he could ever get up there again. He had foresight; with rejuvenation just getting started, he had a whole flock of ideas about overpopulation and the need for a Mars Colony—he was all wet on the population angle, of course, but nobody knew that then. He kicked Keller and Lijinsky off on the Starship idea. They admit it—it was MAN ON MARS that first started them thinking. They were both young, with lots of fight in them. Okay?"

"Just stick to facts," said Dan coldly.

*

"Okay. Starship Project got started, and blossomed into the people's Baby. They started work on the basic blueprints about 60 years ago. Everybody knew it would be a long job—cost money, plenty of it, and there was so much to do before the building ever began. That was where I came in, fifteen years ago. Building. They were looking for engineers who weren't

32

eager to get rich. It went fine. We started to build. Then Keller and Stark came back from rejuvenation. Lijinsky had been rejuvenated five years before."

"Look, I don't need a course in history," Dan exploded.

"Yes, you do," Paul snapped. "You need to sit down and listen for once, instead of shooting your big mouth off all the time. That's what you need real bad, Dan." Paul Fowler rubbed his chin. There were red spots in his cheeks. "Okay, there were some changes made. I didn't like the engine housing—I never had, so I went along with them a hundred percent on that. Even though I designed it—I'd learned a few things since. And there were bugs. It made perfectly good sense, talking to Lijinsky. Starship Project was pretty important to all of us. Dangerous to risk a fumble on the first play, even a tiny risk. We might never get another chance. Lijinsky knew we youngsters were driving along on adrenalin and nerves, and couldn't wait to get out there, but when you thought about it, what was the rush? Was it worth a chance of a fumble to get out there *this* year instead of *next*? Couldn't we take time to find a valid test for that engine at ultra-high acceleration before we put it back in? After all, we *had* time now—Keller and Stark just back with sixty more years to live—why the rush?

"Okay. I bought it. We worked out a valid test on paper. Took us four years of work on it to find out you couldn't build such a device on Earth, but never mind that. Other things were stalling all the while. The colony-plan for the ship. Choosing the crew—what criteria, what qualifications? There was plenty of time—why not make *sure* it's right? Don't leave anything crude, if we can refine it a little first—"

MARTYR

Paul sighed wearily. "It snowballed. Keller and Stark backed Lijinsky to the hilt. There was some trouble about money—I think you had your thumb in the pie there, getting it fixed for us, didn't you? More refining. Work it out. Detail. Get sidetracked on some aspect for a few years—so what? Lots of time. Rejuvenation, and all that, talk about the Universalists beating Rinehart out and throwing the Center open to everybody. Et cetera, et cetera. But somewhere along the line I began to see that it just wasn't true. The holdups, the changes, the digressions and snags and refinements were all excuses, all part of a big, beautiful, exquisitely reasonable facade built up to obscure the real truth. *Lijinsky and Keller and Stark had changed.*"

Dan Fowler snorted. "I know a very smart young doctor who told me that there *weren't* any changes."

"I don't mean anything physical—their bodies were fine. Nothing mental, either—they had the same sharp minds they always had. It was a change in values. They'd lost something that they'd had before. The *drive* that made them start Starship Project, the *urgency*, the vital importance of the thing—it was all gone. They just didn't have the push any more. They began to look for the easy way, and it was far easier to build and rebuild, and refine, and improve the Starship here on the ground than to throw that Starship out into space—"

*

There was a long, long silence. Dan Fowler sat grey-faced, staring at Paul, just shaking his head and staring. "I don't believe it," he said finally. "You do maybe, because you want to, but you're mixed up, Paul. I've seen Lijinsky's reports. There's been progress, regular progress, month by month. You've been

34

too close to it, maybe. Of course there have been delays, but only when they were necessary. The progress has gone on—"

Paul stood up suddenly. "Come in here, Dan. Look." He threw open a door, strode rapidly down a corridor and a flight of stairs into the long, low barn of a laboratory. "Here, here, let me show you something." He pulled out drawers, dragged out rolls of blueprints. "These are my own. They're based on the working prints from Starship that we drew up ten years ago, scaled down to model size. I've tested them, I've run tolerances, I've checked the math five ways and back again. I've tested the parts, the engine—model size. The blueprints haven't got a flaw in them. They're perfect as they'll ever get. No, wait a minute, look—"

He strode fiercely across to slide back a floor panel, drew up the long, glittering thing from a well in the floor—sleek, beautiful, three feet long. Paul maneuvered a midget loading crane, guided the thing into launching position on the floor, then turned back to Dan. "There it is. Just a model, but it's perfect. Every detail is perfect. There's even fuel in it. No men, but there could be if there were any men small enough."

Anger was blazing in Paul's voice now, bitterness and frustration. "I built it, because I had to be sure. I've tested its thrust. I could launch this model for Alpha Centauri tonight—and *it would get there.* If there were little men who could get into it, *they'd* get there, too—alive. Starship Project is completed, it's been completed for ten years now, but do you know what happened to these blueprints, the originals? They were studied. They were improvements. They almost had the ship built, and then they took it apart again."

"But I've read the reports," Dan cried.

MARTYR

"Have you *seen* the Starship? Have you *talked* to them over there? It isn't just there, it's *everywhere*, Dan. There are only about 70,000 rejuvenated men alive in this hemisphere so far, but already the change is beginning to show. Go talk to the Advertising people—*there's* a delicate indicator of social change if there ever was one. See what they say. Who are they backing in the Government? You? Like hell. Rinehart? No, they're backing up 'Moses' Tyndall and his Abolitionist goon-squad who preach that rejuvenation is the work of Satan, and they're giving him enough strength that he's even getting *you* worried. How about Roderigo Aviado and his Solar Energy Project down in Antarctica? Do you know what he's been doing down there lately? You'd better find out, Dan. What's happening to the Mars Colony? Do you have any idea? You'd better find out. Have you gone to see any of the Noble Ten that are still rattling around? Oh, you ought to. How about all the suicides we've been having in the last ten years? What do the insurance people say about that?"

*

He stopped, from lack of breath. Dan just stared at him, shaking his head like Silly Willy on the teevies. "Find out what you're doing, Dan—before you push this universal rejuvenation idea of yours through. Find out—if you've got the guts to find out, that is. We've got a monster on our hands, and now you've got to be Big Dan Fowler playing God and turning him loose on the world. Well, be careful. Find out first, while you can. It's all here to see, if you'll open your eyes, but you're all so dead sure that you want life everlasting that nobody's even bothered to *look*. And now it's become such a political bludgeon that nobody *dares* to look."

The model ship seemed to gleam in the dim laboratory light. Dan Fowler walked over to it, ran a finger up the shiny side to the pinpoint tip. His face was old, and something was gone from his eyes when he turned back to Paul. "You've known this for so long, and you never told me. You never said a word." He shook his head slowly. "I didn't know you hated me so much. But I'm not going to let you win this one, either, Paul. You're wrong. I'm going to prove it if it kills me."

V

"Well, try his home number, then," Dan Fowler snarled into the speaker. He gnawed his cigar and fumed as long minutes spun off the wall clock. His fingers drummed the wall. "How's that? Dammit, I want to speak to Dwight McKenzie, his aide will *not* do—well, of course he's in town. I just saw him yesterday—"

He waited another five minutes, and then his half dollar clanked back in the return, with apologies. "All right, get his office when it opens, and call me back." He reeled off the number of the private booth.

Carl Golden looked up as he came back to the table and stirred sugar-cream into half-cold coffee. "No luck?"

"Son of a bitch has vanished." Dan leaned back against the wall, glowering at Carl and Jean. Through the transparent walls of the glassed-in booth, they could see the morning breakfast-seekers drifting into the place. "We should have him pretty soon." He bit off the end of a fresh cigar, and assaulted it with a match.

"Dad, you know what Dr. Moss said—"

MARTYR

"Look, little girl—if I'm going to die in ten minutes, I'm going to smoke for those ten minutes and enjoy them," Dan snapped. The coffee was like lukewarm dishwater. Both the young people sipped theirs with bleary early-morning resignation. Carl Golden needed a shave badly. He opened his second pack of cigarettes. "Did you sleep on the way back?"

Dan snorted. "What do you think?"

"I think Paul might be lying to you."

Dan shot him a sharp glance. "Maybe—but I don't think so. Paul has always been fussy about telling the truth. He's all wrong, of course—" (fresh coffee, sugar-cream)—"but I think *he* believes his tale. Does it sound like he's lying to you?"

Carl sighed and shook his head. "No. I don't like it. It sounds to me as though he's pretty sure he's right."

Dan clanked the cup down and swore. "He's demented, that's what he is! He's waited too long, his brain's starting to go. If that story of his were true, why has he waited so long to tell somebody about it?"

"Maybe he wanted to see you hang yourself."

"But I can only hang myself on facts, not on the paranoid ramblings of a sick old man. The horrible thing is that he probably believes it—he almost had me believing it, for a while. But it isn't true. He's wrong—good lord, he's *got* to be wrong." Dan broke off, staring across at Carl. He gulped the last of the coffee. "If he *isn't* wrong, then that's all, kiddies. The mountain sinks into the sea, with us just ten feet from the top of it."

"Well, would *you* walk into the Center for a Retread now without being sure he's wrong?"

"Of course I wouldn't," said Dan peevishly. "Paul has taken the game right out from under our noses. We've got to stop everything and find out *now*, before we do another damned thing." The Senator dragged a sheaf of yellow paper out of his breast pocket and spread it out on the table. "I worked it out on the way back. We've got a nasty job on our hands. More than we can possibly squeeze in before the Hearing come up on December 15th. So number one job is to shift the Hearings back again. I'll take care of that as soon as I can get McKenzie on the wire."

"What's your excuse going to be?" Jean wanted to know.

"Anything but the truth. McKenzie thinks I'm going to win the fight at the Hearings, and he wants to be on the right side of the toast when it's buttered. He'll shift the date back to February 15th. Okay, next step: we need a crew. A crowd that can do fast, accurate, hard work and not squeal if they don't sleep for a month or so. Tommy Sandborn should be in Washington—he can handle statistics for us. In addition, we need a couple of good sharp detectives. Jean?"

*

The girl nodded. "I can handle that end. It'll take some time getting them together, though."

"How much time?"

"Couple of days."

"Fine, we can have lots of work for them in a couple of days." The Senator turned back to Carl. "I want you to hit Starship Project first thing."

Carl shook his head. "I've got a better man for that job. Saw him last night, and he's dying for something to do. You don't know him—Terry Fisher. He'll know how to dig out what we want. He was doing it for five years on Mars."

39

"The alky?" Dan didn't like it. "We can't risk a slip to the teevies. We just don't dare."

"There won't be any slip. Terry jumped in the bottle to get away from Mars, that's all. He'll stay cold when it counts."

"Okay, if you say so. I want to see the setup there, too, but I want it ready for a quick scan. Get him down there this morning to soften things up and get it all out on the table for me. You'd better tackle the ad-men, then. Let's see—Tenner's Agency in Philly is a good place to start. Then hit Metro Insurance. Don't waste time with underlings, go to the top and wave my name around like an orange flag. They won't like it a damned bit, but they know I have the finger on Kornwall in Communications. We'll take his scalp if they don't play ball. All you'll have to do is convince them of that."

"What's on Kornwall?"

"Kornwall has been fronting for 'Moses' Tyndall for years. That's why Tyndall never bothered me too much, because we could get him through Kornwall any time we wanted to. And the ad-men and Metro have everything they own sunk into Tyndall's plans." Carl's frown still lingered. "Don't worry about it, son. It's okay."

"I think maybe you're underestimating John Tyndall."

"Why?"

"I worked for him once, remember? He doesn't like you. He knows it's going to be you or him, in the long haul, with nobody else involved. And you realize what happens if 'Moses' gets wind of this mess? Finds out what your brother told you, or even finds out that you're worried about something?"

Dan chewed his lip. "He *could* be a pain, couldn't he?"

"He sure could. More than a pain, and Kornwall wouldn't be much help after the news got out."

"Well, we'll have to take the risk, that's all. We'll have to be fast and quiet." He pushed aside his coffee cup as the phone blinker started in. "I think that gets us started. Jean, you'll keep somebody on the switchboard, and keep track of us all. When I get through with McKenzie, I may be leaving the country for a while. You'll have to be my ears, and cover for me. *Yes*, yes. I was calling Dwight McKenzie—"

The phonebox squawked for a moment or two.

"Hello, Dwight?—What? Oh, thunder! Well, where is he? Timagami—Ontario? An island!" He covered the speaker and growled, "He's gone moose-hunting." Then: "Okay, get me Eastern Sea-Jet Charter Service."

Five minutes later they walked out onto the street and split up in three different directions.

*

A long series of grey, flickering pictures, then, for Dan Fowler. A fast meal in the car to the Charter Service landing field. Morning sun swallowed up, sky gray, then almost black, temperature dropping, a grey drizzling rain. Cold. Wind carrying it across the open field in waves, slashing his cheeks with icy blades of water. Grey shape of the ski-plane ("Eight feet of snow up there, according to the IWB reports. Lake's frozen three feet thick. Going to be a rough ride, Senator"). Jean's quick kiss before he climbed up, the sharp worry in her eyes ("Got your pills, Dad? Try to sleep. Take it easy. Give me a call about anything—") (But there aren't any phones, the operator said. Better not tell her that. Why scare her any more? Damned heart, anyway). A wobbly takeoff that almost dumped his stomach in his lap, sent the briefcase flying across the cabin. Then rain, and grey-black nothing out through the mid-day view ports, heading north. Faster, faster, why can't you get this crate to move? Sorry, Senator. Nasty currents up here. Maybe we can try going higher—

Time! Paul had called it more precious than life, and now time flew screaming by in great deadly sweeps, like a black-winged buzzard. And through it all, weariness, tiredness that he had never felt before. Not years, not work. Weary body, yes—and time was running out, he should have rejuvenated years ago. But now—*what if Paul were right?*

Can't do it now. Not until Paul is wrong, a thousand times wrong. That was it, of course, that was the weariness that wasn't time-weariness or body-weariness. Just mind-weariness. Weariness at the thought of wasted work, the wasted years—a wasted life. Unless Paul is very wrong.

A snarl of disgust, a toggle switch snapped, a flickering teevie screen. Wonderful pickup these days. News of the World brought to you by Atomics International, the fuel to power the Starship—the President returned to Washington today after three-week vacation conference in Calcutta with Chinese and Indian dignitaries—full accord and a cordial ending to the meeting—American medical supplies to be made available—and on the home front, appropriations renewed for Antarctica Project, to bring solar energy into every home, Aviado was quoted as saying—huge Abolitionist rally last night in New Chicago as John 'Moses' Tyndall returned to that city to celebrate the fifteenth birthday of the movement that started there back in 2119—no violence reported as Tyndall lashed out at Senator Daniel Fowler's universal rejuvenation program—twenty-five hour work week hailed by Senator Rinehart of Alaska as a great progressive step for the American people—Senator Rinehart, chairman of the policy-making Criterion Committee held forth hope last night that rejuvenation techniques may increase the number of candidates to six hundred a year within five years—and now, news from the entertainment world—

Going down, then, into flurries of Northern snow, peering out at the whiter gloom below, a long stretch of white with blobs of black on either side, resolving into snow-laden black pines, a long flat lake-top of ice and snow. Taxi-ing down, engines roaring, sucking up snow into steam in the orange afterblast. And ahead, up from the lake, a black blot of a house, with orange window lights reflecting warmth and cheer against the wilderness outside—

Then Dwight McKenzie, peering out into the gloom, eyes widening in recognition, little mean eyes with streaks of fear through them, widening and then smiling, pumping his hand. "Dan! My god, I couldn't *imagine*—hardly ever see anybody up here, you know. Come in, come in, you must be half frozen. What's happened? Something torn loose down in Washington?" And more questions, fast, tumbling over each other, no answers wanted, talky-talk questions to cover surprise and fear and the one large question of why Dan Fowler should be dropping down out of the sky on *him*, which question he didn't think he wanted answered just yet—

*

A huge, rugged room, blazing fire in a mammoth fireplace at the end, moose heads, a rug of thick black bear hide. "Like to come up here a day or two ahead of the party, you know,"

MARTYR

McKenzie was saying. "Does a man good to commune with his soul once in a while. Do you like to hunt? You should join us, Dan. Libby and Donaldson will be up tomorrow with a couple of guides. We could find you an extra gun. They say hunting should be good this year—"

One chair against the fireplace, a book hastily thrown down beside it, SEXTRA SPECIAL, Cartoons by Kulp. Great book for soul-searching Senators. Things were all out of focus after the sudden change from the cold, but now Dan was beginning to see. One book, one chair, but two half-filled sherry glasses at the sideboard—

"Can't wait, Dwight, I have to get back to the city, but I couldn't find you down there, and they didn't know when you were coming back. I just wanted to let you know that I put you to all that trouble for nothing—we don't need the Hearing date in December, after all."

Wariness suddenly in McKenzie's eyes. "Well! Nice of you to think of it, Dan—but it wasn't really any trouble. No trouble at all. December 15th is fine, as a matter of fact, better than the February date would have been. Give the Committee a chance to collect itself during the Holidays, ha, ha."

"Well, it now seems that it *wouldn't* be so good for me, Dwight. I'd much prefer it to be changed back to the February date."

"Well, now." Pause. "Dan, we *have* to settle these things sooner or later, you know. I don't know whether we can do that now—"

"Don't know! Why not?"

The moose-hunter licked both lips, couldn't keep his eyes on Dan's eyes, focused on his nose instead,—as if the nose were

44

really the important part of the conversation. "It isn't just me that makes these decisions, Dan. Other people have to be consulted. It's pretty late to catch them now, you know. It might be pretty hard to do that—"

No more smiles from Dan. "Now look—you make the calendar, and you can change it." Face getting red, getting angry—careful, Dan, those two sherry glasses, watch what you say—"I want it changed back. And I've got to know right now."

"But you told me you'd be all ready to roll by December 15th—"

To hell with caution—he *had* to have time. "Look, there's no reason you can't do it if you want to, Dwight. I'd consider it a personal favor—I repeat, a very large personal favor—if you'd make the arrangements. I won't forget it—" What did the swine want, an arm off at the roots?

"Sorry," said a voice from the rear door of the room. Walter Rinehart walked across to the sideboard. "You don't mind if I finish this, Dwight?"

A deep breath from McKenzie, like a sigh of relief. "Go right ahead, Walt. Sherry, Dan?"

"No, I don't think so." It was Walter, all right. Tall, upright, dignified Walter, fine shock of wavy hair that was white as the snow outside. Young-old lines on his face. Some men looked finer after rejuvenation, much finer than before. There had been a chilly look about Walter Rinehart's eyes before his first Retread. Not now. A fine man, like somebody's dear old grandfather. Just give him a chunk of wood to whittle and a jack-blade to whittle it with—

MARTYR

But inside, the mind was the same. Inside, no changes. Author of the Rinehart Criteria, the royal road to a self-perpetuating "immortal elite."

*

Dan turned his back on Rinehart and said to McKenzie: "I want the date changed."

"I—I can't do it, Dan." An inquiring glance at Rinehart, a faint smiling nod in return.

He knew he'd blundered then, blundered badly. McKenzie was afraid. McKenzie wanted another lifetime, one of these days. He'd decided that Rinehart would be the one who could give it to him. But worse, far worse: Rinehart knew now that something had happened, something was wrong. "What's the matter, Dan?" he said smoothly. "You need more time? Why? You had it before, and you were pretty eager to toss it up. Well, what's happened, Dan?"

That was all. Back against the wall. The thought of bluffing it through, swallowing the December 15th date and telling them to shove it flashed through his mind. He threw it out violently, his heart sinking. That was only a few more days. They had weeks of work ahead of them. They needed more time, they *had* to have it—

Rinehart was grinning confidently. "Of course I'd like to cooperate, Dan. Only I have some plans for the Hearings, too. You've been getting on people's nerves, down in the city. There's even been talk of reconsidering your rejuvenation permit—"

Your move, Dan. God, what a blunder! Why did you ever come up here? And every minute you stand there with your jaw sagging just tells Rinehart how tight he's got you—*do* something, *anything*—

There was a way. Would Carl understand it? Carl had begged him never to use it, ever, under any circumstances. And Carl had trusted him when he had said he wouldn't—but if Carl were standing here now, he'd say yes, go ahead, use it, wouldn't he? He'd have to—

"I want the Hearings on February 15th," Dan said to Rinehart.

"Sorry, Dan. We can't be tossing dates around like that. Unless you'd care to tell me why."

"Okay." Dan grabbed his hat angrily. "I'll make a formal request for the change tomorrow morning, and read it on the teevies. Then I'll also announce a feature attraction that the people can look forward to when the Hearing date comes. We weren't planning to use it, but I guess you'd like to have both barrels right in the face, so that's what we'll give you."

Walter Rinehart roared with laughter. "*Another* feature attraction? You do dig them up, don't you? Ken Armstrong's dead, you know."

"Peter Golden's widow isn't."

*

The smile faded on Rinehart's face. He looked suddenly like a man carved out of grey stone. Dan trembled, let the words sink in. "You didn't think *anybody* knew about that, did you, Walt? Sorry. We've got the story on Peter Golden. Took us quite a while to piece it together, but we did with the help of his son. Carl remembers his father before the accident, you see, quite well. His widow remembers him even before that. And we have some fascinating recordings that Peter Golden made when he applied for rejuvenation, and when he appealed the

47

Committee's decisions. Some of the private interviews, too, Walter."

"I gave Peter Golden forty more years of life," Rinehart said.

"You crucified him," said Dan, bluntly.

There was silence, long silence. Then: "Are you selling?"

"I'm selling." Cut out my tongue, Carl, but I'm selling.

"How do I know you won't break it anyway?"

"You don't know. Except that I'm telling you I won't."

Rinehart soaked that in with the last gulp of sherry. Then he smashed the glass on the stone floor. "Change the date," he said to McKenzie. "Then throw this vermin out of here."

Back in the snow and darkness Dan tried to breathe again, and couldn't quite make it. He had to stop and rest twice going down to the plane. Then he was sick all the way back.

VI

Early evening, as the plane dropped him off in New York Crater, and picked up another charter. Two cold eggs and some scalding coffee, eaten standing up at the airport counter. Great for the stomach, but there wasn't time to stop. Anyway, Dan's stomach wasn't in the mood for dim lights and pale wine, not just this minute. Questions howling through his mind. The knowledge that he had made the one Class A colossal blunder of his thirty years in politics, this last half-day. A miscalculation of a man! He should have known about McKenzie—at least suspected. McKenzie was getting old, he wanted a Retread, and wanted it badly. Before, he had planned to get it through Dan. Then something changed his mind, and he decided Rinehart would end up on top.

Why?

Armstrong's suicide, of course. Pretty good proof that even Rinehart hadn't known it was a suicide. If Carl had brought back evidence of murder, Dan would win, McKenzie thought. But evidence of suicide—it was shaky. Walt Rinehart has his hooks in too deep.

They piped down the fifteen minute warning for the Washington Jet. Dan gulped the last of his coffee, and found a visi-phone booth with a scrambler in working order. Two calls. The first one to Jean, to line up round-the-clock guards for Peter Golden's widow on Long Island. Jean couldn't keep surprise out of her voice. Dan grunted and didn't elaborate—just get them out there.

Then a call to locate Carl. He chewed his cigar nervously.

Two minutes of waiting while they called Carl from wherever he was. Then: "I just saw McKenzie. I found him hiding in Rhinehart's hip pocket."

"Jesus, Dan. We've got to have time."

"We've got it—but the price was very steep, son."

Silence then as Carl peered at him. Finally: "I see."

"If I hadn't been in such a hurry, if I'd only thought it out," Dan said miserably. "It was an awful error—and all mine, too."

"Well, don't go out and shoot yourself. I suppose it had to happen sooner or later. What about Mother?"

"She'll be perfectly safe. They won't get within a mile of her. Look, son—is Fisher doing all right?"

Carl nodded. "I talked to him an hour ago. He'll be ready for you by tomorrow night, he thinks."

"Sober?"

MARTYR

"Sober. And mad. He's the right guy for the job." Worried lines deepened on Golden's forehead. "Everything's O.K.? Rinehart won't dare—"

"I scared him. He'd almost forgotten. Everything's fine." Dan rang off, scowling. He wished he was as sure as he sounded. Rinehart's back was to the wall, now. Dan wasn't too sure he liked it that way.

An hour later he was in Washington, and Jean was dragging him into the Volta. "If you don't sleep now, I'll have you put to sleep. Now shut up while I drive you home."

A soft bed, darkness, escape. When had he slept last? It was heaven.

*

He slept the clock around, which he had not intended, and caught the next night-jet to Las Vegas, which he had intended. There was some delay with the passenger list after he had gone aboard, a fight of some sort, and the jet took off four minutes late. Dan slept again, fitfully.

Somebody slid into the adjoining seat. "Well! Good old Dan Fowler!"

A gaunt, frantic-looking man, with skin like cracked parchment across his high cheekbones, and a pair of Carradine eyes looking down at Dan. If Death should walk in human flesh, Dan thought, it would look like John Tyndall.

"What do you want, 'Moses'?"

"Just dropped by to chat," said Tyndall. "You're heading for Las Vegas, eh? Why?"

Dan jerked, fumbled for the upright-button. "I like the climate out there. If you want to talk, talk and get it over with."

Tyndall lifted a narrow foot and gave the recline-button a sharp jab, dumping the Senator back against the seat. "You're onto something. I can smell it cooking, and I want my share, right now."

Dan stared into the gaunt face, and burst out laughing. He had never actually been so close to John Tyndall before, and he did *not* like the smell, which had brought on the laugh, but he knew all about Tyndall. More than Tyndall himself knew, probably. He could even remember the early rallies Tyndall had led, feeding on the fears and suspicions and nasty rumors grown up in the early days. It was evil, they had said. This was not God's way, this was Man's way, as evil as Man was evil. If God had wanted Man to live a thousand years, he would have given him such a body—

Or:

They'll use it for a tool! Political football. They'll buy and sell with it. They'll make a cult of it, they're doing it right now! Look at Walter Rinehart. Did you hear about his scheme? To keep it down to five hundred a year? They'll make themselves a ruling class, an immortal elite, with Rinehart for their Black Pope. Better that *nobody* should have it—

Or:

Immortality, huh? But what kind? You hear what happened to Harvey Tatum? That's right, the jet-car man, big business. He was one of their 'Noble Ten' they're always bragging about. But they say he had to have special drugs every night, that he had *changed*. That's right, if he didn't get these drugs, see, he'd go mad and try to suck blood and butcher up children—oh, they didn't dare publish it, had to put him out of the way quietly, but my brother-in-law was down in Lancaster one night when—

MARTYR

*

All it really needed was the man, and one day there was 'Moses' Tyndall. Leader of the New Crusade for God. Small, at first. But the ad-men began supporting him, broadcasting his rallies, playing him up big. Abolish rejuvenation, it's a blot against Man's immortal soul. Amen. Then the insurance people came along, with money. (The ad-men and the insurance people weren't too concerned about Man's immortal soul—they'd take their share now, thanks—but this didn't bother Tyndall too much. Misguided, but they were on God's side. He prayed for them.) So they gave Tyndall the first Abolitionist seat in the Senate, in 2124, just nine years ago, and the fight between Rinehart and Dan Fowler that was brewing even then had turned into a three-cornered fight—

*

Dan grinned up at Tyndall and said, "Go away, John. Don't bother me."

"You've got something," Tyndall snarled. "What is that damn shadow of yours nosing around Tenner's for? Why the sudden leaping interest in Nevada? Two trips in three days—what are you trying to track down?"

"Why on Earth should I tell you anything, Holy Man?"

The parchment face wrinkled unpleasantly. "Because it would be very smart, that's why. Rinehart's out of it, now. Washed up, finished, thanks to you. Now it's just you or me, one or the other. You're in the way, and you're going to be gotten out of the way when you've finished up Rinehart, because I'm going to start rolling them. Go along with me now and you won't get smashed, Dan."

"Get out of here," Dan snarled, sitting bolt upright. "You gave it to Carl Golden, a long time ago when he was with you, remember? Carl's my boy now—do you think I'll swallow the same bait?"

"You'd be smart if you did." The man leaned forward. "I'll let you in on a secret. I've just recently had a—*vision*, you might say. There are going to be riots and fires and shouting, around the time of the Hearings. People will be killed. Lots of people—spontaneous outbursts of passion, of course, the great voice of the people rising against the Abomination. And against *you*, Dan. A few Repeaters may be taken out and hanged, and then when you have won against Rinehart, you'll find people thinking that you're really a traitor—"

"Nobody will swallow that," Dan snapped.

"Just watch and see. I can still call it off, if you say so." He stood up quickly as Dan's face went purple. "New Chicago," he said smoothly. "Have to see a man here, and then get back to the Capitol. Happy hunting, Dan. You know where to reach me."

He strode down the aisle of the ship, leaving Dan staring bleakly at an empty seat.

Paul, Paul—

*

He met Terry Fisher at the landing field in Las Vegas. A firm handshake, clear brown eyes looking at him the way a four-year-old looks at Santa Claus. "Glad you could come tonight, Senator. I've had a busy couple of days. I think you'll be interested." Remarkable restraint in the man's voice. His face was full of things unsaid. Dan caught it; he knew faces, read them like typescript. "What is it, son?"

MARTYR

"Wait until you see." Fisher laughed nervously. "I thought for a while that I was back on Mars."

"Cigar?"

"No thanks. I never use them."

The car broke through darkness across bumpy pavement. The men sat silently. Then a barbed-wire enclosure loomed up, and a guard walked over, peered at their credentials, and waved them through. Ahead lay a long, low row of buildings, and a tall something spearing up into the clear desert night. They stopped at the first building, and hurried up the steps.

Small, red-faced Lijinsky greeted them, all warm handshake and enthusiasm and unmistakable happiness and surprise. "A real pleasure, Senator! We haven't had a direct governmental look-see in quite a while. I'm glad I'm here to show you around."

"Everything is going right along, eh?"

"Oh, yes! She'll be a ship to be proud of. Now, I think we can arrange some quarters for you for the night, and in the morning we can sit down and have a nice, long talk."

Terry Fisher was shaking his head. "I think the Senator would like to see the ship now—isn't that right, Senator?"

Lijinsky's eyes opened wide, his head bobbed in surprise. Young-old creases on his face flickered. "Tonight? Oh, you can't really be serious. Why, it's almost two in the morning! We only have a skeleton crew working at night. Tomorrow you can see—"

"Tonight, if you don't mind." Dan tried to keep the sharp edge out of his voice. "Unless you have some specific objection, of course."

54

"Objection? None whatsoever." Lijinsky seemed puzzled, and a little hurt. But he bounced back: "Tonight it is, then. Let's go." There was no doubting the little man's honesty. He wasn't hiding anything, just surprised. But a moment later there was concern on his face as he led them out toward the factory compounds. "There's no question of appropriations, I hope, Senator?"

"No, no. Nothing of the sort."

"Well, I'm certainly glad to hear that. Sometimes our contacts from Washington are a little disappointed in the Ship, of course."

Dan's throat tightened. "Why?"

"No reason, really. We're making fine progress, it isn't that. Yes, things really buzz around here; just ask Mr. Fisher about *that*—he was here all day watching the workers. But there are always minor changes in plans, of course, as we recognize more of the problems."

Terry Fisher grimaced silently, and followed them into a small Whirlwind groundcar. The little gyro-car bumped down the road on its single wheel, down into a gorge, then out onto the flats. Dan strained his eyes, peering ahead at the spear of Starship gleaming in the distant night-lights. Pictures from the last Starship Progress Report flickered through his mind, and a frown gathered as they came closer to the ship. Then the car halted on the edge of the building-pit and they blinked down and up at the scaffolded monster.

Dan didn't even move from the car. He just stared. The report had featured photos, projected testing dates—even ventured a possible date for launching, with the building of the Starship so near to completion. That had been a month ago. Now Dan stared at the ship and shook his head, uncomprehending.

The hull-plates were off again, lying in heaps on the ground in a mammoth circle. The ship was a skeleton, a long, gawky structure of naked metal beams. Even now a dozen men were scampering around the scaffolding, before Dan's incredulous eyes, and he saw some of the beaming coming *off* the body of the ship, being dropped onto the crane, moving slowly to the ground.

Ten years ago the ship had looked the same. As he watched, he felt a wave of hopelessness sweep through him, a sense of desolate, empty bitterness. Ten years—

His eyes met Terry Fisher's in the gloom of the car, begging to be told it wasn't so. Fisher shook his head.

Then Dan said: "I think I've seen enough. Take me back to the air field."

*

"It was the same thing on Mars," Fisher was telling him as the return jet speared East into the dawn. "The refining and super-refining, the slowing down, the changes in viewpoint and planning. I went up there ready to beat the world barehanded, to work on the frontier, to build that colony, and maybe lead another one. I even worked out the plans for a break-away colony—we would need colony-builders when we went to the stars, I thought." He shrugged sadly. "Carl told you, I guess. They considered the break-away colony, carefully, and then Barness decided it was really too early. Too much work already, with just one colony. And there was, in a sense: frantic activity, noise, hubbub, hard work, fancy plans—all going nowhere. No drive, no real direction." He shrugged again. "I did a lot of drinking before they threw me off Mars."

"Nobody saw it happening?"

"It wasn't the sort of thing you see. You could only *feel* it. It started when Armstrong came to the colony, rejuvenated, to take over its development. And eventually, I think Armstrong did see it. That's why he suicided."

"But the Starship," Dan cried. "It was almost built, and they were *tearing it down*. I saw it with my own eyes."

"Ah, yes. For the twenty-seventh time, I think. A change in the engineering thinking, that's all. Keller and Lijinsky suddenly came to the conclusion that the whole thing might fall apart in midair at the launching. Can you imagine it? When rockets have been built for years, running to Mars every two months? But they could prove it on paper, and by the time they got through explaining it every damned soul on the project was saying yes, it might fall apart at the launching. Why, it's a standing joke with the workers. They call Keller "Old Jet Propulsion" and always have a good laugh. But then, Keller and Stark and Lijinsky should know what's what. They've all been rejuvenated, and working on the ship for years." Fisher's voice was heavy with anger.

Dan didn't answer. There didn't seem to be much *to* answer, and he just couldn't tell Fisher how it felt to have a cold blanket of fear wrapping around his heart, so dreadful and cold that he hardly dared look five minutes ahead right now. *We have a Monster on our hands—*

MARTYR

VII

He was sick when they reached Washington. The pain in his chest became acute as he walked down the gangway, and by the time he found a seat in the terminal and popped a nitro-tablet under his tongue he was breathing in deep, ragged gasps. He sat very still, trying to lean back against the seat, and quite suddenly he realized that he was very, very ill. The good red-headed Dr. Moss would smile in satisfaction, he thought bitterly. There was sweat on his forehead; it had never seemed very probable to him that he might one day die—he didn't *have* to die in this great, wonderful world of new bodies for old, he could live on, and on, and on. He could live to see the Golden Centuries of Man. A solar system teeming with life. Ships to challenge the stars, the barriers breaking, crumbling before their very eyes. Other changes, as short-lived Man became long-lived Man. Changes in teaching, in thinking, in feeling. Disease, the Enemy, was crushed. Famine, the Enemy, slinking back into the dim memory of history. War, the Enemy, pointless to extinction.

All based on one principle: Man must live. He need not die. If a man could live forty years instead of twenty, had it been wrong to fight the plagues that struck him down in his youth? If he could live sixty years instead of forty, had the great researchers of the 1940's and '50's and '60's been wrong? Was it any more wrong to want to live a thousand years? Who could say that it was?

He took a shuddering breath, and then nodded to Terry Fisher, and walked unsteadily to the cab stand. He would not believe what he had seen at Starship Project. It was not enough. Collect the evidence, *then* conclude. He gave Fisher an ashen smile. "It's nothing. The ticker kicks up once in a while, that's all. Let's go see what Carl and Jean and the boys have dug up." Fisher smiled grimly, an eager gleam in his eye.

Carl and Jean and the boys had dug up plenty. The floor of offices Dan rented for the work of his organization was going like Washington Terminal at rush hour. A dozen people were here and there, working with tapes, papers, program cards. Jean met them at the door, hustled them into the private offices in the back. "Carl just got here, too. He's down eating. The boys outside are trying to make sense out of his insurance and advertising figures."

"He got next to them okay?"

"Sure—but you were right, they didn't like it."

"What sort of reports?"

*

The girl sighed. "Only prelims. Almost all of the stuff is up in the air, which makes it hard to evaluate. The ad-men have to be figuring what they're going to do next half-century, so that they'll be there with the right thing when the time comes. But it seems they don't like what they see. People have to buy what the ad-men are selling, or the ad-men shrivel up, and already the trend seems to be showing up. People aren't in such a rush to buy. Don't have the same sense of urgency that they used to—" Her hands fluttered. "Well, as I say, it's all up in the air. Let the boys analyze for a while. The suicide business is a little more tangible. The rates are up, all over. But break it into first-generation and Repeaters, and it's pretty clear who's pushing it up."

"Like Armstrong," said Dan slowly.

Jean nodded. "Oh, here's Carl now."

MARTYR

He came in, rubbing his hands, and gave Dan a queer look. "Everything under control, Dan?"

Dan nodded. He told Carl about Tyndall's proposition. Carl gave a wry grin. "He hasn't changed a bit, has he?"

"Yes, he has. He's gotten lots stronger."

Carl scowled, and slapped the desk with his palm. "You should have stopped him, Dan. I told you that a long time ago—back when I first came in with you. He was aiming for your throat even then, trying to use me and what I knew about Dad to sell the country a pack of lies about you. He almost did, too. I hated your guts back then. I thought you were the rottenest man that ever came up in politics, until you got hold of me and pounded sense into my head. And Tyndall's never forgiven you that, either."

"All right—we're still ahead of him. Have you just finished with the ad-men?"

"Oh, no. I just got back from a trip south. My nose is still cold."

Dan's eyebrows went up. "And how was Dr. Aviado? I haven't seen a report from Antarctica Project for five years."

"Yes you have. You just couldn't read them. Aviado is quite a theoretician. That's how he got his money and his Project, down there, with plenty of room to build his reflectors and nobody around to get hurt if something goes wrong. Except a few penguins. And he's done a real job of development down there since his rejuvenation."

"Ah." Dan glanced up hopefully.

"Now there," said Carl, "is a real lively project. Solar energy into power on a utilitarian level. The man is fanatic, of course, but with his plans he could actually be producing in another five years." He lit a cigarette, drew on it as though it were bitter.

"Could?"

"Seems he's gotten sidetracked a bit," said Carl.

Dan glanced at Terry Fisher. "How?"

"Well, his equipment is working fine, and he can concentrate solar heat from ten square miles onto a spot the size of a manhole cover. But he hasn't gone too far converting it to useful power yet." Carl suddenly burst out laughing. "Dan, this'll kill you. Billions and billions of calories of solar heat concentrated down there, and what do you think he's doing with it? He's digging a hole in the ice two thousand feet deep and a mile wide. That's what."

"A hole in the ice!"

"Exactly. Conversion? Certainly—but first we want to be sure we're right. So right now his whole crew is very busy *trying to melt down Antarctica*. And if you give him another ten years, he'll have it done, by god."

*

This was the last, most painful trip of all.

Dan didn't even know why he was going, except that Paul had told him he should go, and no stone could be left unturned.

The landing in New York Crater had been rough, and Dan had cracked his elbow on the bulkhead; he nursed it now as he left the Volta on the deserted street of the crater city, and entered the low one-story lobby of the groundscraper. The clerk took his name impassively, and he sat down to wait.

An hour passed, then another.

Then: "Mr. Devlin will see you now, Senator."

MARTYR

Down in the elevator, four—five—six stories. Above him was the world; here, deep below, with subtly efficient ventilators and shafts and exotic cubby-holes for retreat, a man could forget that a world above existed.

Soft lighting in the corridor, a golden plastic door. The door swung open, and a tiny old man blinked out.

"Mr. Chauncey Devlin?"

"Senator Fowler!" The little old man beamed. "Come in, come in—my dear fellow, if I'd realized it was you, I'd never have dreamed of keeping you so long—" He smiled, obviously distressed. "Retreat has its disadvantages, too, you see. Nothing is perfect but life, as they say. When *you've* lived for a hundred and ninety years, you'll be glad to get away from people, and to be able to keep them out, from time to time."

In better light Dan stared openly at the man. A hundred and ninety years. It was incredible. He told the man so.

"Isn't it, though?" Chauncey Devlin chirped. "Well, I was a was-baby! Can you imagine? Born in London in 1945. But I don't even think about those horrid years any more. Imagine—people dropping bombs on each other!"

A tiny bird of a man—three times rejuvenated, and still the mind was sharp, the eyes were sharp. The face was a strange mixture of recent youth and very great age. It stirred something deep inside Dan—almost a feeling of loathing. An uncanny feeling.

"We've always known your music," he said. "We've always loved it. Just a week ago we heard the Washington Philharmonic doing—"

"The eighth." Chauncey Devlin cut him off disdainfully. "They always do the eighth."

"It's a great symphony," Dan protested.

Devlin chuckled, and bounced about the room like a little boy. "It was only half finished when they chose me for the big plunge," he said. "Of course I was doing a lot of conducting then, too. Now I'd much rather just write." He hurried across the long, softly-lit room to the piano, came back with a sheaf of papers. "Do you read music? This is just what I've been doing recently. Can't get it quite right, but it'll come, it'll come."

"Which will this be?" asked Dan.

"The tenth. The ninth was under contract, of course—strictly a pot-boiler, I'm afraid. Thought it was pretty good at the time, but *this* one—ah!" He fondled the smooth sheets of paper. "In this one I could *say* something. Always before it was hit and run, make a stab at it, then rush on to stab at something else. Not *this* one." He patted the manuscript happily. "With this one there will be _nothing_ wrong."

"It's almost finished?"

"Oh, no. Oh, my goodness no! A fairly acceptable first movement, but not what I *will* do on it—as I go along."

"I see. I—understand. How long have you worked on it now?"

"Oh, I don't know—I must have it down here somewhere. Oh, yes. Started it in April of 2057. Seventy-seven years."

They talked on, until it became too painful. Then Dan rose, and thanked his host, and started back for the corridor and life again. He had never even mentioned his excuse for coming, and nobody had missed it.

Chauncey Devlin, a tiny, perfect wax-image of a man, so old, so wise, so excited and full of enthusiasm and energy and carefulness, working eagerly, happily—

MARTYR

Accomplishing nothing. Seventy-seven years. The picture of a man who had been great, and who had slowly ground to a standstill.

And now Dan knew that he hadn't really been looking at Chauncey Devlin at all. He had been looking at the whole human race.

VIII

February 15th, 2135.

The day of the Hearings, to consider the charges and petition formally placed by The Honorable Daniel Fowler, Independent Senator from the Great State of Illinois. The long oval hearing-room was filling early; the gallery above was packed by 9:05 in the morning. Teevie-boys all over the place. The Criterion Committee members, taking their places in twos and threes—some old, some young, some rejuvenated, some not, taking their places in the oval. Then the other Senators—not the President, of course, but he'll be well represented by Senator Rinehart himself, ah yes. Don't worry about the President.

*

Bad news in the papers. Trouble in New Chicago, where so much trouble seems to start these days. Bomb thrown in the Medical Center out there, a *bomb* of all things! Shades of Lenin. Couple of people killed, and one of the doctors nearly beaten to death on the street before the police arrived to clear the mob away. Dan Fowler's name popping up here and there, not pleasantly. Whispers and accusations, *sotto voce*. And 'Moses' Tyndall's network hookup last night—of course nobody with any sense listens to *him*, but did you hear that hall go wild?

Rinehart—yes, that's him. Well, he's got a right to look worried. If Dan can unseat him here and now, he's washed up. According to the rules of the Government, you know, Fowler can legally petition for Rinehart's chairmanship without risking it as a platform plank in the next election, and get a hearing here, and then if the Senate votes him in, he's got the election made. Dan's smart. They're scared to throw old Rinehart out, of course—after all, he's let them keep their thumbs on rejuvination all these years with his Criteria, and if they supported him they got named, and if they didn't, they didn't get named. Not quite as crude as that, of course, but that's what it boiled down to, let me tell you! But now, if they reject Dan's petition and the people give him the election over their heads, they're *really* in a spot. Out on the ice on their rosy red—

How's that? Can't be too long now. I see Tyndall has just come in, Bible and all. See if he's got any tomatoes in his pockets. Ol' Moses really gets you going—ever listen to him talk? Well, it's just as well. Damn, but it's hot in here—

In the rear chamber, Dan mopped his brow, popped a pill under his tongue, dragged savagely on the long black cigar. "You with me, son?"

Carl nodded.

"You know what it means."

"Of course. There's your buzzer. Better get in there." Carl went back to Jean and the others around the 80-inch screen, set deep in the wall. Dan put his cigar down, gently, as though he planned to be back to smoke it again before it went out, and walked through the tall oak doors.

*

MARTYR

The hubbub caught, rose up for a few moments, then dropped away. Dan took his seat, grinned across at Libby, leaned his head over to drop an aside into Parker's ear. Rinehart staring at the ceiling as the charges are read off in a droning voice—

—*Whereas the criteria for selection of candidates for sub-total prosthesis, first written by the Honorable Walter Rinehart of the Great State of Alaska, have been found to be inadequate, outdated, and utterly inappropriate to the use of sub-total prosthesis that is now possible—*

—*And whereas that same Honorable Walter Rinehart has repeatedly used the criteria, not in the just, honorable, and humble way in which such criteria must be regarded, but rather as a tool and weapon for his own furtherance and for that of his friends and associates—*

Dan waited, patiently. Was Rinehart's face whiter than it had been? Was the Hall quieter now? Maybe not—but wait for the petition—

—*The Senate of the United States of North America is formally petitioned that the Honorable Walter Rinehart should be displaced from his seat as Chairman in the Criterion Committee, and that his seat as Chairman of that committee should be resumed by the Honorable Daniel Fowler, author of this petition, who has hereby pledged himself before God to seek through this Committee in any and every way possible, the extention of the benefits of sub-total prosthesis techniques to all the people of this land and not to a chosen few—*

Screams, hoots, cat-calls, applause, all from the gallery. None below—Senatorial dignity forbade, and the anti-sound glass kept the noise out of the chamber below. Then Dan Fowler stood up, an older Dan Fowler than most of them seemed to remember.

"You have heard the charges which have been read. I stand before you now, formally, to withdraw them—"

What, what? Jaws sagging, eyes wide; teevie camera frozen on the Senator's face, then jerking wildly around the room to catch the reaction—

"You have also heard the petition which has been read. I stand before you now, formally, to withdraw it—"

Slowly, measuring each word, he told them. He knew that words were not enough, but he told them. "Only 75,000 men and women have undergone the process, at this date, out of almost two hundred million people on this continent, yet it has already begun to sap our strength. We were told that no change was involved, and indeed we saw no change, but it was there, my friends. The suicides of men like Kenneth Armstrong did not just *occur*. There are many reasons that might lead a man to take his life in this world of ours—selfishness, self-pity, hatred of the world or of himself, bitterness, resentment—but it was none of these that motivated Kenneth Armstrong. *His death was the act of a bewildered, defeated mind*—for he saw what I am telling you now and knew that it was true. He saw Starships built and rebuilt, and never launched—colonies dying of lethargy, because there was no longer any drive behind them—brilliant minds losing sight of goals, and drifting into endless inconsequential digressions—lifetimes wasted in repetition, in re-doing and re-writing and re-living. He saw it: the downward spiral which could only lead to death for all of us in the last days.

"This is why I withdraw the charges and petition of this Hearing. This is why I reject rejuvenation, and declare that it is a monstrous thing *which we must not allow to continue*. This is why I now announce that I personally will nominate the

MARTYR

Honorable John Tyndall for President in the elections next spring, and will promise him my pledged support, my political organization and experience, and my every personal effort to see that he is elected."

*

It seemed that there would be no end to it, when Dan Fowler had finished. 'Moses' Tyndall had sat staring as the blood drained out of his sallow face; his jaw gaped, and he half-rose from his chair, then sank back with a ragged cough, staring at the Senator as if he had been transformed into a snake. Carl and Terry were beside Dan in a moment, clearing a way back to the rear chambers, then down the steps of the building to a cab. Senator Libby intercepted them there, his face purple with rage, and McKenzie, bristling and indignant. "You've lost your mind, Dan."

"I have not. I am perfectly sane."

"But *Tyndall*! He'll turn Washington into a grand revival meeting, he'll—"

"Then we'll cut him down to size. He's *my* candidate, remember, not his own. He'll play my game if it pays him well enough. But I want an Abolitionist administration, and I'm going to get one."

In the cab he stared glumly out the window, his heart racing, his whole body shaking in reaction now. "You know what it means," he said to Carl for the tenth time.

"Yes, Dan, I know."

"It means no rejuvenation, for you or for any of us. It means proving something; to people that they just don't want to believe, and cramming it down their throats if we have to. It means taking away their right to keep on living."

"I know all that."

"Carl, if you want out—"

"Yesterday was the time."

"Okay then. We've got work to do."

IX

Up in the offices again, Dan was on the phone immediately. He knew politics, and people—like the jungle cat knows the whimpering creatures he stalks. He knew that it was the first impact, the first jolting blow that would win for them, or lose for them. Everything had to hit right. He had spent his life working with people, building friends, building power, banking his resources, investing himself. Now the time had come to cash in.

Carl and Jean and the others worked with him—a dreadful afternoon and evening, fighting off newsmen, blocking phone calls, trying to concentrate in the midst of bedlam. The campaign to elect Tyndall had to start *now*. They labored to record a work-schedule, listing names, outlining telegrams, drinking coffee, as Dan swore at his dead cigar like old times once again, and grinned like a madman as the plans slowly developed and blossomed out.

Then the phone jangled, and Dan reached out for it. It was that last small effort that did it. A sledge-hammer blow, from deep within him, sharp agonizing pain, a driving hunger for the air that he just couldn't drag into his lungs. He let out a small, sharp cry, and doubled over with pain. They found him seconds later, still clinging to the phone, his breath so faint as to be no breath at all.

*

MARTYR

He regained consciousness hours later. He stared about him at the straight lines of the ceiling, at the hospital bed and the hospital window. Dimly he saw Carl Golden, head dropping on his chest, dozing at the side of the bed.

There was a hissing sound, and he raised a hand, felt the tiny oxygen mask over his mouth and nose. But even with that help, every breath was an agony of pain and weariness.

He was so very tired. But slowly, through the fog, he remembered. Cold sweat broke out on his forehead, drenched his body. *He was alive.* Yet he remembered crystal clear the thought that had exploded in his mind in the instant the blow had come. *I'm dying. This is the end—it's too late now.* And then, cruelly, *why did I wait so long?*

He struggled against the mask, sat bolt upright in bed. "I'm going to die," he whispered, then caught his breath. Carl sat up, smiled at him.

"Lie back, Dan. Get some rest."

Had he heard? Had Carl heard the fear he had whispered? Perhaps not. He lay back, panting, as Carl watched. Do you know what I'm thinking, Carl? I'm thinking how much I want to live. People don't *need* to die—wasn't that what Dr. Moss had said? It's such a terrible waste, he had said.

Too late, now. Dan's hands trembled. He remembered the Senators in the oval hall, hearing him speak his brave words; he remembered Rinehart's face, and Tyndall's, and Libby's. He was committed now. Yesterday, no. Now, yes.

Paul had been right, and Dan had proved it.

His eyes moved across to the bedside table. A telephone. He was still alive, Moss had said that sometimes it was possible *even when you were dying.* That was what they did with your father, wasn't it, Carl? Brave Peter Golden, who had fought Rinehart so hard, who had begged and pleaded for universal rejuvenation, waited and watched and finally caught Rinehart red-handed, to prove that he was corrupting the law and expose him. Simple, honest Peter Golden, applying so naively for his rightful place on the list, when his cancer was diagnosed. Peter Golden had been all but dead when he had finally whispered defeat, and given Rinehart his perpetual silence in return for life. They had snatched him from death, indeed. But he had been crucified all the same. They had torn away everything, and found a coward underneath.

Coward? Why? Was it wrong to want to live? Dan Fowler was dying. Why must it be him? He had committed himself to a fight, yes, but there were others, young men, who could fight. Men like Peter Golden's son.

But you are their leader, Dan. If you fail them, they will never win.

Carl was watching him silently, his lean dark face expressionless. Could the boy read his mind? Was it possible that he knew what Dan Fowler was thinking? Carl had always understood before. It had seemed that sometimes Carl had understood Dan far better than Dan did. He wanted to cry out to Carl now, spill over his dreadful thoughts.

There was no one to run to. He was facing himself now. No more cover-up, no deceit. Life or death, that was the choice. No compromise. Life or death, but decide *now*. Not tomorrow, not next week, not in five minutes—

He knew the answer then, the flaw, the one thing that even Paul hadn't known. That life is too dear, that a man loves life—not what he can *do* with life, but very life itself for its own sake—too much to die. It was no choice, not really. A man will *always* choose life, as long as the choice is really his. Dan Fowler knew that now.

It would be selling himself—like Peter Golden did. It would betray Carl, and Jean, and all the rest. It would mean derision, and scorn, and oblivion for Dan Fowler.

Carl Golden was standing by the bed when he reached out his arm for the telephone. The squeaking of a valve—what? Carl's hand, infinitely gentle, on his chest, bringing up the soft blankets, and his good clean oxygen dwindling, dwindling—

Carl!

How did you know?

*

She came in the room as he was reopening the valve on the oxygen tank. She stared at Dan, grey on the bed, and then at Carl. One look at Carl's face and she knew too.

Carl nodded, slowly. "I'm sorry, Jean."

She shook her head, tears welling up. "But you loved him so."

"More than my own father."

"Then *why?*"

"He wanted to be immortal. Always, that drove him. Greatness, power—all the same. Now he will be immortal, because we needed a martyr in order to win. Now we will win. The other way we would surely lose, and he would live on and on, and die every day." He turned slowly to the bed and brought the sheet up gently. "This is better. This way he will never die."

They left the quiet room.

www.ingramcontent.com/pod-product-compliance
Lightning Source LLC
Chambersburg PA
CBHW050904120626
46554CB00003B/999